Snowed In

by *Barbara M. Lucas*
illustrated by Catherine Stock

Bradbury Press   New York
Maxwell Macmillan Canada   Toronto
Maxwell Macmillan International
New York   Oxford   Singapore   Sydney

A NOTE ABOUT THE ART

The illustrations for *Snowed In* were done on Waterford paper using watercolors.
Research was done at the New York Public Library and was influenced by Elinore Pruitt Stewart's
Letters of a Woman Homesteader, University of Nebraska Press, Lincoln, 1961. The illustrations
were color-separated by scanner and reproduced in four colors using red, blue, yellow, and black inks.

Bradbury Press
Macmillan Publishing Company
866 Third Avenue
New York, NY 10022

Maxwell Macmillan Canada, Inc.
1200 Eglinton Avenue East
Suite 200
Don Mills, Ontario M3C 3N1

Macmillan Publishing Company is part of the Maxwell Communication Group of Companies.

First edition
Printed and bound in Hong Kong by South China Printing Company (1988) Ltd.
10 9 8 7 6 5 4 3 2 1
The text of this book is set in Garamond #3.
Typography by Julie Quan

LIBRARY OF CONGRESS CATALOGING-IN-PUBLICATION DATA
Lucas, Barbara M.
Snowed in / by Barbara M. Lucas ; illustrated by Catherine Stock.
—1st ed.
p.   cm.
Summary: Snowed in for the winter at their Wyoming frontier home in the early twentieth
century and unable to attend school, Grace and Luke keep busy reading, studying, singing, and sharing stories.
ISBN 0-02-761465-4
[1. Snow—Fiction.] I. Stock, Catherine, ill. II. Title.
PZ7.L9686Sn 1993
[E]—dc20   92-39081

*In memory of
Rae Marie and
Jarod Michael Warren*
—B. M. L.

For Harry
—C. S.

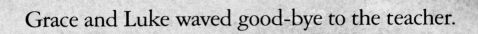

Grace and Luke waved good-bye to the teacher.

They rode to the store in Father's wagon.

"We need paper and pencils," Father said to the
storekeeper. "And plenty of them."

Father drove his wagon to the library.

"We need books," Father said to the librarian. "And plenty of them."

Father filled one box with books. Grace took *The Legend of Sleepy Hollow* down from a shelf. She and Luke filled another box with books.

"Home we go," Father said.

As the wagon pulled up at the house, snow began to fall.

By next morning snowdrifts covered the road.

"We are snowed in for the winter," Mother said.

"Here are pencils, paper, and books," Father
said. "And plenty of them."
　　He helped Grace and Luke with their
numbers.

Mother read the stories they wrote and
checked the spelling.

At night Father popped corn on the stove.

Luke sang "Home on the Range."

Grace asked her favorite riddle: "What has eyes all over it but can't see a thing?"

No one guessed the right answer.

"A potato!" Grace told them.

They all laughed at that.

Everyone read the books.

Weeks later, warm spring days arrived. The snowdrifts melted.

Luke and Grace helped Father return the
library books.

They ran to the schoolhouse. Grace and Luke
were happy to see their friends. At school they
learned new numbers and words.

"We have good teachers," Grace said.
Luke added, "And plenty of them."